This book belongs to:

_____

_____

_____

First published 2008 by Walker Books Ltd
87 Vauxhall Walk, London SE11 5HJ

2 4 6 8 10 9 7 5 3 1

© 2008 Lucy Cousins
Lucy Cousins font © 2008 Lucy Cousins

The author/illustrator has asserted her moral rights

"Maisy" audio visual series produced by King Rollo Films Ltd
for Universal Pictures International Visual Programming

Maisy™. Maisy is a registered trademark of Walker Books Ltd, London

Printed in Singapore

British Library Cataloguing in Publication Data:
a catalogue record for this book is
available from the British Library

ISBN 978-1-4063-1336-9

www.walkerbooks.co.uk

Maisy Goes to the Museum

Lucy Cousins

WALKER BOOKS
AND SUBSIDIARIES
LONDON · BOSTON · SYDNEY · AUCKLAND

They all like the
museum very much.

First everyone wanted to see the dinosaur. What enormous bones! And look at the fossilised dinosaur's egg!

EGG

T-REX

In the transport section, Charley loved the vintage car...

and the penny farthing bicycle...

and the double-decker bus!

What a wonderful
old biplane!
And look
here,
a satellite,
and a rocket!

Maisy imagines being an astronaut and flying to the moon with Panda.

Everyone enjoyed
the old toys.

Tallulah's favourite
was the grand
doll's house with
all its tiny
furniture.

In the natural history section, Maisy and Charley marvelled at the brightly coloured birds.

INSECTS

Tallulah inspected the insects.

Cyril made friends with
the sabre-toothed tiger.

And Eddie looked and looked at the dear old woolly mammoth.

There's so much
to see and do
at the museum.

You can draw...

play with puppets...

make music...

and dress up in the costume room. Maisy dressed up as an Egyptian.

Cyril was a knight.
Look at his shining armour.

"Now it's time to visit the food section!" Charley said.

So they went to the museum café and had delicious cakes and refreshing drinks.

"There's always something new to see at the museum," Maisy said on the way home.

"And there's always something old to see," said Eddie.